CIRCUS
in the Sky

Written by

Nancy Guettier

Illustrated by

Gina Kil

Chiami Sekine

Keny Kim

James

Designed by

Abeck Inc.

This book is dedicated to my son Julian.
A little boy with a big imagination and appreciation
for the night sky and its magical mysteries.

Every night Julian is tucked
in his cozy bed, but he is never tired.

So Julian asks his dad to read
him two books, then three.
"I promise I'll go to sleep after
the fourth," Julian says.

When his dad is done,
Julian pretends to sleep.
His dad gives him a gentle kiss
on the head, tiptoes out the room
and says, "Sweet dreams."

Julian slowly opens his eyes and stares up
at his ceiling covered with glow-in-the-dark
stickers of stars.

He dreams
he is the ringleader
of the circus in
the sky.

The circus tent hangs
from the stars, floating
way up high.

And then he shouts:
The greatest show is about to begin!
The 88 constellations patiently await
and if you watch closely you will
appreciate the brightest acts.
You will be amazed! Just stop and
look up at the sky and gaze.

The Seven Sisters
start the opening dance…

...while Mighty Archer takes his stance.

Pegasus

The carousel turns and spins with delight
with Pegasus' wings so magnificently bright.

Cygnus

Aquila

Delphinus

Around and round it
goes with Delphinus, Cygnus
and Aquila in a row.

Cassiopeia sits sideways in her chair,
while we all are still with wonder and stare.

The Gemini twins are always a delight,
walking on the tightrope, stepping in unison.
So light, so bright!

Then mighty Leo
roars with all his might.
His heart, known
as Regulus, beating
just right.

Ursa Major

Ursa Minor

Ursa Minor and Major
begin their act,
rolling and tumbling
to distract.

Then Draco
the Dragon spews
fire for all of
us to admire.

Draco

Perseus

Andromeda

Freed by Perseus, the hero of the sky, Andromeda breaks from her chains. She is free to fly!

The stars of the circus radiate the stage
in hopes that we will all engage.

And if you couldn't sleep
and missed tonight's show,
close your eyes and dream—
they'll be back tomorrow.

Seven Sisters

Mighty Archer

Pegasus

Delphinius

Cygnus

Leo

Aquila

Ursa Major & Ursa Minor

Cassiopeia

Draco

Twins

Perseus & Andromeda

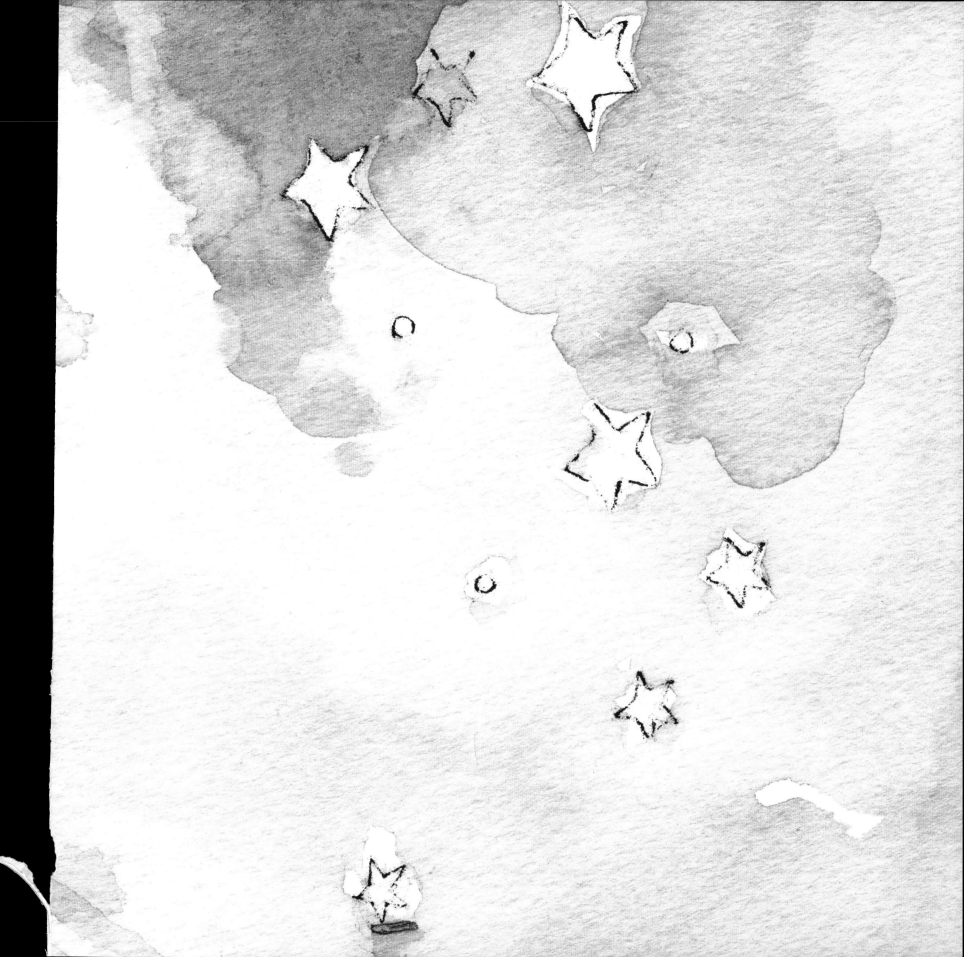

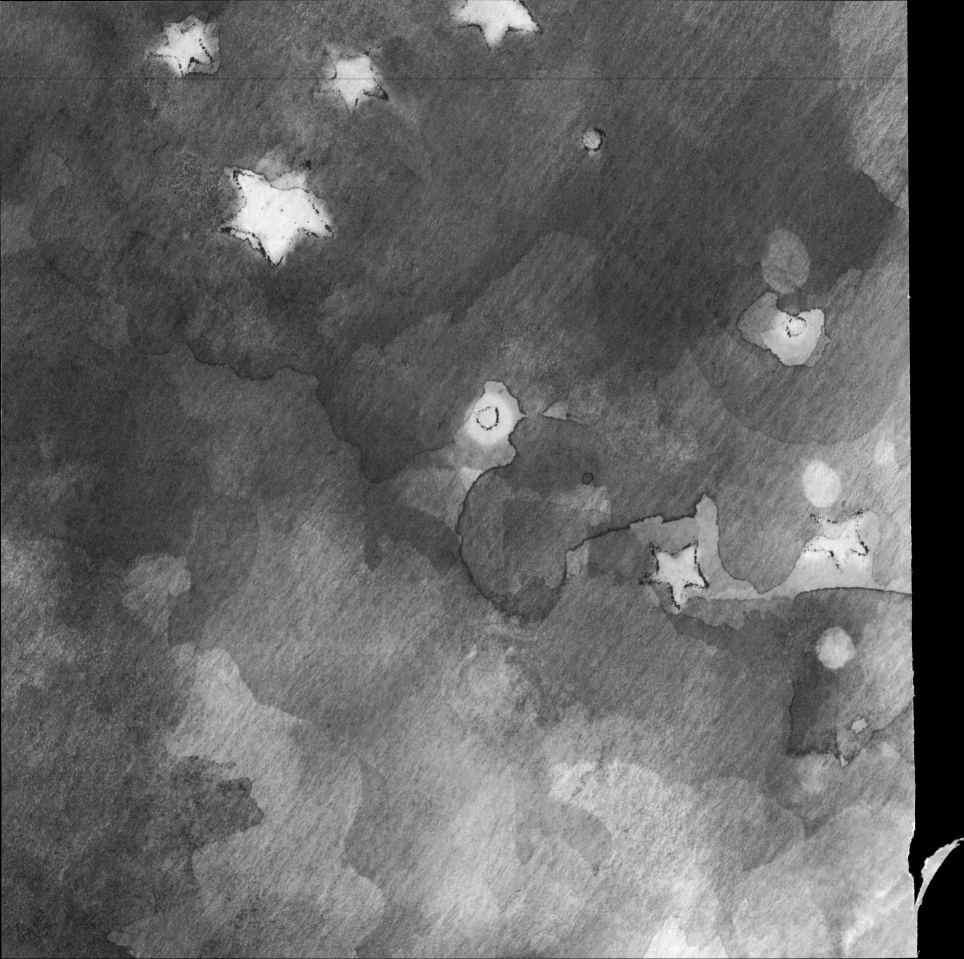